This book belongs to: BB♡

To Carme Solé Vendrell
and the mountain

This paperback edition first published in 2020 by Andersen Press Ltd.

First published in Great Britain in 1985 by Andersen Press Ltd.,

20 Vauxhall Bridge Road, London SW1V 2SA.

Copyright © David McKee, 1985.

The right of David McKee to be identified as the author

and illustrator of this work has been asserted by him

in accordance with the Copyright, Designs and Patents Act, 1988.

All rights reserved.

Colour separated in Switzerland by Photolitho AG, Zürich.

Printed and bound in China.

1   3   5   7   9   10   8   6   4   2

British Library Cataloguing in Publication Data available.

ISBN 978 1 84270 831 6

TWO MONSTERS

David McKee

ANDERSEN PRESS

There was once a monster that lived quietly
on the west side of the mountain.

On the east side of the mountain
lived another monster.

Sometimes the monsters spoke together
through a hole in the mountain.

But they never saw each other.

One evening the first monster called through the hole, "Can you see how beautiful it is? Day is departing."

"Day departing?" called back the second monster. "You mean night arriving, you twit!"

"Don't call me a twit, you dumbo, or I'll get angry," fumed the first monster and he felt so annoyed that he could hardly sleep.

The other monster felt just as irritated
and he slept very badly as well.

The next morning the first monster felt awful after such a bad night. He shouted through the hole, "Wake up, you numbskull, night is leaving."

"Don't be stupid, you peabrain!" answered the second. "That is day arriving." And with that he picked up a stone and threw it over the mountain.

"Rotten shot, you big ignoramus!" called the first monster as the stone missed him. He picked up a bigger stone and hurled it back.

That stone also missed. "Hopeless, you hairy, no-neck nerk!" howled the second monster, and he threw back a rock which knocked the top off the mountain.

"You're just a stupid old wind-filled prune!"
shouted the first monster as he heaved a boulder
that knocked another piece off the mountain.

"And you're a revolting, soggy cornflake!" replied the second monster. This time he kicked a huge rock just for a change.

As the day passed the rocks grew bigger and bigger and the insults grew longer and longer.

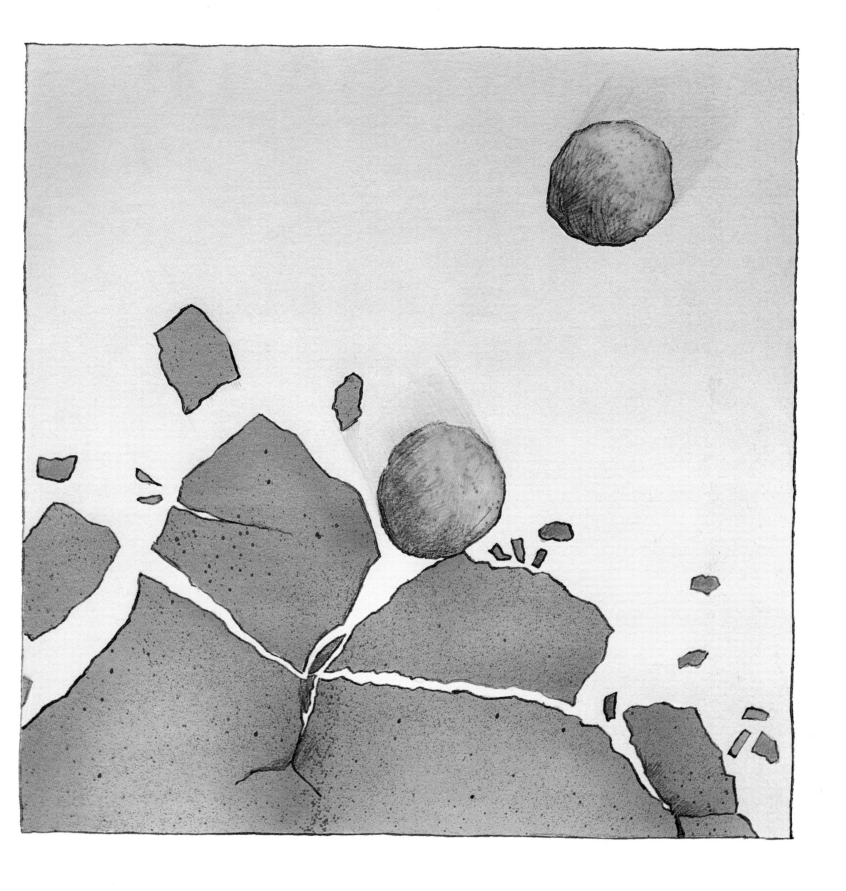

Both of the monsters remained untouched but
the mountain **was** being knocked to pieces.

"You're a hairy, overstuffed, empty-headed, boggly-eyed mess!" shouted the first monster as he threw yet another massive boulder.

"You're a pathetic, addlebrained, smelly, lily-livered custard tart!" screamed the second monster hurling a yet larger rock.

That rock finally smashed the last of the mountain and for the very first time the monsters saw each other.

This happened just at the beginning
of another sunset.

"Incredible," said the first monster putting
down the rock he was holding.
"There's night arriving. You were right."

"Amazing," gasped the second monster
dropping his boulder.
"You are right, it is day leaving."

They walked to the middle of the mess they had made to watch the arrival of the night and the departure of the day together.

"That was rather fun," giggled the first monster.
"Yes, wasn't it," chuckled the second.
"Pity about the mountain."

More books by David McKee: